THE LITTLE COTTAGE BY THE SEA

A.L. Jambor

Woofie

Woofie

Cover design by: Amy Jambor
Photo Credits: Viviamo@depositphotos.com

For Jeff and Paul

CONTENTS

PROLOGUE

1855

Though the fierce wind battered the cottage out on Barrington Bluff, the stoic little dwelling was as strong as the man who built her, a sea captain named Colin Brinker, as handsome a man as ever lived, and whose heart was forever drawn to the sea.

There was also a maiden who had won his heart, the fair Molly Barton, who accepted his proposal to wed. She was young and lithe, with a sweet spirit and goodness that endeared her to the villagers who lived in Port Revere.

The lovers wed on a snowy Yuletide Eve, and drove off in a carriage drawn by two white horses. Colin had a horseshoe in his pocket, and a gleam in his eye. Husband and wife consummated their marriage and swore their undying love before drifting off to sleep.

During the night a terrible nor'easter with winds that shook the cottage's foundation and battered the walls so violently that the windows shattered and the shutters were torn asunder. The lovers, however, were unaware of the terrible storm, for a cocoon of love surrounded the pair and kept them safe until morning.

When Colin and Molly awoke the next day, they were surprised to see shards of glass and shattered wood, and thanked the good Lord for delivering them from certain death. To commemorate the event, Colin planted an oak tree the next spring before taking his ship to Bermuda.

Now the villagers would tell the tale for years, embellishing it a bit, but always coming to the same conclusion; that as Colin built the cottage, his love had been sealed within its walls. That love enchanted the cottage, and anyone who lived within its fair walls would be blessed.

1

Present Day

Meg started writing several years ago when Amazon gave independent writers a chance to publish their own books, and she had been moderately successful, but her writing hadn't paid the bills. She'd worked as a staff writer on a magazine until it went bust at the beginning of 2012, and when she received her severance pay, she decided the time had come for her to work full time on her fiction writing. Her first book, a sweeping Victorian romance, made it all the way to number 10 on Amazon's top 100 Historical Romance – Victorian category. She gained a small following and wrote another, and then another, and soon people were asking when her next novel was coming out.

Meg did book signings and mailing lists, wrote a blog, tweeted, Facebooked, and Instagramed. Then her sister, Maddie, died.

After Maddie's death, the thought of sitting in front of a computer made her shake, and stopped going on social media, shut down her blog, and put her laptop under the bed.

Around six months after Maddie passed away, Meg, driven by a desire to reconnect with her past, went to Port Revere on Cape Cod and spent a few days visiting places she and Maddie had gone to during their summer vacations.

She climbed the hill to the cottage on Barrington Bluff and saw a "For Sale" sign on the front lawn. The old place had always stoked Meg's romantic dreams, and she peeked inside the windows, which led to a call to the real estate agent and a down payment. She sold her townhouse in Boston, sold any furniture she couldn't fit into the cottage, and left her old life behind.

Her nephew, Zack, who lived in Oakland, California had come to stay with her for a while when she moved into the cottage on Barrington Bluff. He helped her set it up, put her computer desk in the bedroom underneath a window looking out at the sea, and helped her sort out the things Meg had kept after his mother died.

On a warm summer night before he went back to California, they sat on her porch and talked about Maddie and Meg's childhood, and her decision to buy the cottage.

"Why all the way out here?" he asked. "What's wrong with Boston?"

"I remember this place from when we were kids. It was such a romantic spot, and the story of how it became enchanted always appealed to me."

"So you believe this cottage is enchanted."

"Of course not. You know I don't believe in

things like that, but I'm a writer and I can stretch my imagination." She sighed. "Maybe I thought it would inspire me to write again."

"Do you think you can get in front of the computer now that you're settled?" When she didn't answer, he tried another approach. "How do you feel when you try to write?"

"Pressure. There's so much to do, and you're always afraid you're going to disappoint someone, or they will post something about you, something negative that's hard to refute because it's on the internet."

"And you're gonna let a few cyber bullies keep you from doing what you love?"

"I don't want to. I still have stories to tell and they keep looping around in my mind."

Zack, who lived on the west coast with his boyfriend, Ethan, was well over thirty, had a great job, and was a whiz at social media. His phone kept vibrating, and he'd look to see who it was, but to his credit, he didn't answer the calls. He was sitting on the porch railing with his back against a column and one leg dangling on the side. She marveled at his youthful body and his joints, which were still limber and pain free.

"I couldn't do that," she said.

"What?" he asked.

"Hang my leg over the side like that. My hip would protest madly."

"Oh, come on, Meg, you're not that old."

"I'm old enough."

He smiled. His blue eyes and sandy hair were so like his mother's.

"So, what are you going to do?" he asked.

"Nothing right now. I've gone through dry spells in the past. If I don't force myself, I'll eventually want to write again."

After Zack went home, she threw herself into renovating the cottage, and when it was done she felt proud yet lonely for there was no one to share it with, or show it to. As the holidays approached, she tried to think of ways to occupy herself so she wouldn't fall into a deep depression. She called Zack on weekends, and he didn't seem to mind talking to her for an hour or more.

"I miss you," she said one gloomy November day.

"You can always come and stay with us for a while."

"I know, and I might take you up on that the first time it snows."

Zack frowned. "It is sort of way out there isn't it? Do snow plows even come out there?"

"That's why I bought the SUV," she said.

The picture of her flying down the hill in SUV and careening off the road entered his mind.

"Maybe you should just close this place up until spring."

"Zack, I just moved in. I'll be fine. I'm not that decrepit yet, you know."

"You're not decrepit at all. It's just that there's no one around for miles."

"The town is not that far, and I'll make sure that

the people in town know I'm out here. I will be fine, Zack."

She cried a lot that month, remembering how she'd stayed with Maddie while she went through the end stages of cancer. As bad as it was, it was also the best time they'd had together since they were kids. It was just the two of them, with intermittent visits from Zack and Ethan, and they watched old movies, ate comfort foods, and Maddie told her over and over how happy she was that Meg was with her.

"I'm glad you're here," she said, holding Meg's hand, and looking into her eyes to make sure her baby sister believed her.

Then a terrible convergence of events began when Meg went to Boston for an author's convention. She'd been out of the public eye for a while and kept getting emails from fans who wanted to see her at the convention. Maddie had been going through a good period and had urged Meg to go.

"You'll be back in no time," Maddie said. "Go. You owe it to the people who buy your books."

Maddie lived in Springfield, just an hour and a half from Boston, so Meg decided to go. While she was signing books, her sister passed away. Thankfully, Zack was by Maddie's side, but that didn't assuage the guilt Meg felt. She believed she would never forgive herself for leaving Maddie's side.

"She wouldn't have known you were there, Meg," Zack said when she came to the hospital that night. "She just stopped breathing." He put his arms around her and held her. "You were with her when it counted."

"I should have been there," Meg said between bouts of tears.

"She wanted you to go."

A nurse told Meg that many people die alone. "It's like they wait for their loved ones to leave. I see it all the time."

That had brought Meg some comfort, but the guilt and pain soon turned into depression. Zack stayed for a week to help with the details of Maddie's funeral and estate, but he had to go home when there was an emergency at work. He promised to return, but was unable to until the summer when he came to help her with the cottage.

He was stunned by her appearance. It was as if Meg had aged overnight. Her hair was limp and her complexion sallow. Afraid he might lose her too, he took a short leave of absence so he could "help you with the cottage."

"I have money," Zack said during his stay. "I can help you anytime you need it."

"I can't take money from you."

"Why not? Come on, Meg. Don't give me a hard time if I want to be nice to you."

She'd finally agreed that if she needed help, she'd ask, but in her heart she knew she couldn't. He was Maddie's only child and the idea of taking money from him was unthinkable.

Maddie and Meg's brother Eddie had died two

years before Maddie, leaving Meg alone. She hadn't been there when Eddie died, either, so when she thought about them, she felt like the worst sister who ever lived, and she missed them both terribly. There were no more calls asking her how she was, or memories that only a sibling can share over lunch at a small café. Eddie had always shared her new book postings on Facebook with the caption "Baby sister's new book" added to the posting. Now, no one shared her postings, and it hurt that she hadn't appreciated his kindness while he was still alive.

In the months that followed, her memories became her companions, walking with her along the beach, or sitting with her while she watched a favorite old movie or TV show. She heard their voices and the expressions they'd used, and after a while, she grew eager to mingle with real humans again. She went to town and got to know some of the shopkeepers. They promised to check on her by phone if they didn't see her in town for a while, but she still hadn't written a word.

Now, Christmas was a month away, and Thanksgiving was at the end of the week. She and Maddie had always gotten together for the holiday, and Meg kept the TV off, hoping it would make the holiday go away. It hadn't, and when she was in the supermarket, the crowds reminded her that Thursday was the big day, and now she had no choice but to face it alone.

Meg bought marshmallows, Rice Krispies, and butter to make squares. When she returned from the supermarket, she had a message on the phone from a plumber she'd contacted to have the plumbing refurbished. He told her he would be out there on Saturday afternoon around two.

After making the squares, she put them in the fridge to set and spent the rest of the night watching holiday specials on TV, and trying not to think of the Thanksgiving dinners her family used to have.

2

As we get older, we forget what it was like to awaken on Christmas morning, run downstairs, and find a trove of toys left by an old man whose only objective in life was to make us happy. We forget how we looked under our pillow to find that money had replaced our missing teeth. Battered by reality, we abandon magic, and soon forget how it made us feel. The childhood excitement that sustained us through the long days between Thanksgiving and Christmas became dread as we tried to provide the magic for our own children, so it's hard to discern it when it comes to our door and shakes our hand.

The old gentleman parked his 1928 Ford truck in front of the cottage, and sighed when he slid out of the driver's seat and put his feet on the ground. Gold letters painted on the driver's side door proclaimed that Angus O'Malley, Plumber Extraordinaire had arrived. An old Labrador Retriever sat on the passenger seat and waited for Angus to call him, but the old man shut the door.

"You wait here, boy. I can't greet a new client with a hound at me feet."

While his accent might have softened since he'd

come to America, his Celtic heritage was strong, and today, Angus was on a mission. While Americans celebrated their day of thanks, Angus was going to spend some time with a lonely lady who thought her house needed new pipes, but Angus had been sent by someone who knew what would truly ease her burden.

He looked at the ocean and recalled, as he always did, the day he landed in New York City. He'd traveled alone from County Cork with a special blessing from his dear old mother, a chailín who practiced the old ways, and five dollars in his pocket.

At the time, Angus didn't understand the blessing his mother made, or the effect it would have on those he met, and he thought of her today as he watched the sea, imagining her standing on the shores of his dear, green land and waving to him the way she had when he left Cobh for good. Angus left his homeland at the tender age of sixteen. He ran from hunger and he cried for weeks, for he missed his mother that much. Now, he waved toward the Emerald Isle and thanked his mother for giving him a gift that continued to bless anyone he met.

He looked at the cottage and thought of the last time he'd been there. He rubbed his chin and scowled, for he had forgotten to shave and ladies frowned upon poor grooming. Still, it was a holiday, and he had been tapped for this mission the day before. He tucked his shirt into his pants, and then, satisfied with his appearance, knocked on the cottage door.

Meg heard the knock and wondered who it could be. Her hand was poised in midair as she was just about to sip her coffee, so she put it down and got up. She was still in her nightclothes, so she peeked out the bay window and saw an elderly gentleman wearing a derby who had arrived in an old truck with a sad-looking Lab in the passenger seat. Though he was a stranger, at his age she doubted he could do her much harm, and she felt sorry for the dog. How had the old man gotten that ancient truck up the hill?

She looked at the name on the side of the truck and didn't recognize it as one of the plumbers she'd contacted, but the dog was whining, and she felt how cold it was when she stood by the window. She clutched her robe at the neck and opened the door.

"Good mornin' to you, Miss," Angus said. "I heard you were needin' the services of a plumber."

"Good morning," she said. "I am, yes, but I don't remember calling you."

"No, ma'am, you didn't, but there is a grapevine to consider, and it's a small town. Word spreads fast, and since I happened to be passin' this way, I thought I'd stop by."

Meg looked at the dog, and then at him.

"I see you're lookin' at me old Barney. He's a decent fella, but I don't like to force 'im on anyone."

"He looks cold. Why don't you bring him inside?"

"If it's no trouble."

"It's no trouble at all," she said.

Angus hobbled back to the truck and let Barney

out. The old dog moved just like his master, and Meg suppressed a smile as she watched them come inside. The dog made a beeline to the hearth and lay down in front of it while Angus looked around the room.

"Aye, tis a sweet little cottage."

He walked toward the kitchen as if he knew where he was going and Meg followed. She watched him pressing on the walls and turning on the faucets. The sink was on the back wall near the corner. The sidewall next to that corner was bare. Angus gave special attention to that wall, and Meg watched him place his hands on it and run them over the surface as if he could feel the pipes through the drywall.

"Aye, tis a sweet cottage indeed."

"Can you feel the pipes that way?" Meg asked.

He looked at her and smiled. "I installed 'em meself back in '54."

"Oh, my. You've been working a long time."

"Aye, a long time, but it's a blessing, you know."

He looked past Meg to the bathroom on the other side of the kitchen and pointed his finger.

"That water closet was brought here from England in pieces."

His wistful expression seemed odd to her, but perhaps it was his occupation that led him to find endearing something most people took for granted – good plumbing.

"The man who built this cottage was ahead of his time."

"Do you know if the pipes have been replaced since then?"

"Now that I can't tell you." He rubbed his chin again. "Tis a mystery."

"But that's why I wanted a plumber to come out here, so they could tell me if I needed new pipes."

"Have you noticed any leaks?" he asked.

"Well, no, but…"

"Then I wouldn't be worryin' about it, no I wouldn't. You'll just be makin' yourself sick with worry, that you will."

He left her and whistled for Barney as he walked to the front door. She ran after him and grabbed his arm.

"But you haven't told me anything."

"It's all in the hearin', Missy. I told you all you need to know." He smiled and his eyes twinkled as he tipped his hat. "Here's to better days a-comin'."

Barney was standing beside him and he licked Meg's hand.

"Aye, even Barney can see you're a fair one indeed. Have a good day, and may the good Lord take a likin' to you."

She went to the window and watched the dog climb into the car before his master, and then watched the old truck drive away. She felt sorry for the man, who couldn't possibly do the necessary work any longer.

She went back to her coffee and sipped it as she watched a squirrel run around the yard. The old man was an odd duck, and he hadn't told her anything.

Why had he come, and on Thanksgiving Day no less? Still, it was sort of nice to have someone drop by, even if it was an eccentric old codger with a sad old Lab.

3

After spending a lackluster Thanksgiving alone, Meg thought about going to visit Zack for Christmas. She used her cell phone to search for flights, and then called him to see if he had room for her in his apartment.

"We have plenty of room," he said.

There wasn't a trace of hesitation in his voice, and it made her feel good that he wanted her to come. She'd only met Ethan once, but she'd liked him instantly, and seeing Zack so happy removed all her doubts about his choice. It would be nice to be with them instead of sitting at home missing her family more than she could bear.

After she hung up, Meg decided to go to town and do some shopping. She found a parking spot on the street near an old art gallery. She remembered it from when she was a girl. It had belonged to the same family for over a century, and its presence comforted her. It was nice to know that some things never changed.

The road running down the center of town had been broad, and sometime in the sixties and the town had voted to build a park in the center of town and create a rotary around it for traffic. A tree was brought in every year and decorated the day after Thanksgiving with brightly colored lights and ornaments made by local schoolchildren. Meg thought it looked lovely, and now that she knew she had somewhere to go for Christmas, she enjoyed the festive atmosphere taking over the town.

Music was piped through an audio system built into the deck where the tree sat. Shopkeepers added lights to their windows, and the scent of pine was everywhere. Meg wondered if that was piped in, too.

The crisp air tickled her nose and made her sneeze. It reminded her of the days she'd walked to school with the wind at her back and her brother Eddie flinging snowballs at her and Maddie. The girls' cheeks were always red and their coats wet from Eddie's assaults, and Meg would get at least one earache a year because she didn't like to wear a hat or cover her ears.

Now, though, she always wore a scarf pulled up high around her ears, gloves, and a thick coat with a sweater underneath. It felt colder than it had fifty years ago, and her hands and feet were always freezing. The twinges she'd been having in her knees and hips were turning into aches, but otherwise she was in good health, a comfort because both her siblings had died from cancer. She got all her wellness checkups, took a mild blood pressure pill, and so far, had avoided the scourge that had decimated her family.

The gallery was at the end of a row of shops

that had been built side by side, each with a large window and a door with a transom. The shops also bore the same gold lettering, done by a local artist, and signs hung so that pedestrians could read them as they walked on the sidewalk underneath them. The gallery also had a window on the side of the building.

She ran from the car to the gallery and felt a blast of hot air when she opened the door. Whoever ran the place kept it nice and cozy, and Meg began peeling layers off as she wandered around the small building that showed the works of local artists both past and present. A diminutive woman appeared at the back of the room and approached Meg with a smile.

"Hello," she said.

"Hi."

"Are you in Port Revere for the day?" the woman asked.

"No, I live here. I bought the Christmas Cottage."

The woman's eyes lit up. "Oh, so you're the author. I'm so happy to meet you, and I was so jealous when I heard you'd bought the cottage. It was always my dream to own it." The lady's smile was warm. "My name is Irma. Would you like a cup of tea?"

"That sounds wonderful."

Meg studied Irma's physical features for future reference as she followed her to the back of the gallery. She would make an interesting character. Irma was quite small, perhaps five foot, with snow-white hair and clear blue eyes. Her dress reflected another era, which might be something she did for the holidays, but it suited her. She resembled a pixie Meg had been given as a child, and she'd put it on her Christmas tree every year.

"I have a table back here next to the hearth and I bought some cakes at the bakery."

Irma took her to a small table with two chairs placed against the wall underneath the side window. Meg threw her coat over the back of her chair, sat, and watched Irma go through a door. Soon she returned with a tray carrying a teapot, cups and saucers, and a plate of petit fours.

"I can't get warm enough this time of year," Irma said. "I hope the fire isn't too hot for you."

"I'm fine. It's cozy."

"That's what I was going for." Irma smiled again. "So, tell me what it's like to live in that old place."

"So far so good. I'm a bit disappointed I haven't seen any ghosts yet, though."

"Are there ghosts in the Christmas Cottage?"

"We used to think there were when we were kids."

Irma smiled. "We often heard stories of good things that happened to anyone who lived there, but I never heard of any ghosts." She poured the tea. "Now, my brother and I used to go up there to camp out now and then. We drove Beulah Brown nearly crazy. We'd peek in her windows and run before she could catch us."

"My sister and I did the same thing, only the

lady's name was Mary Spencer. We would camp close enough so she wouldn't see us until daylight, then she would chase us with a broom and we'd laugh all the way home, but we never saw so much as a misty figure and we were so disappointed."

"Gee, I hadn't thought about my brother in years." Irma was quiet for a moment. "He died in the big war."

"I'm so sorry."

"So, you lived around here before?"

"Only during the summer. My folks rented a place on Liberty Street."

Irma squinted. "What was your last name?"

"Osborne. My dad was Kenneth Osborne."

"Oh, yes, I remember him. Nice looking fellow."

"I always thought so."

"And I remember your mother, too. She and I used to go to the same beauty parlor. Always got a permanent, but we called them temporaries."

Irma laughed, and Meg nodded.

"Mom always got her hair done, and sprayed it so much that when my nephew touched it, he asked her why she had paper hair."

Irma laughed again. "Oh, I hadn't thought of Sarah in so long. So many of my friends are gone now."

They were quiet for a long time with only the sound of the crackling fire to intrude upon their reverie. The tea grew cold and the cakes were consumed while they both thought of people who were gone, and then Irma narrowed her eyes.

"Didn't you have a brother and sister?"

"Yes, but they have both passed away."

"Oh, dear, and so young. I'm so sorry."

"It's been hard. I think losing a sibling is worse than losing a parent."

Irma tilted her head. "I never stopped missing my brother."

Meg nodded. She felt herself tearing up, and Irma saw the tears glistening in her eyes.

"You know, I think I have something you might be interested in, but we have to go upstairs."

Meg followed Irma through the door at the back of the room where a small kitchenette with a sink and hot plate had been installed. She wondered if the fire department knew about that hot plate as she followed Irma to a narrow staircase. Irma switched on the overhead light and Meg worried that the elderly woman would miss a step, but Irma was spry and walked up them like a teenager. When they got to the top, Meg saw a railing and on the other side, an attic full of discarded artwork.

"Most people have to bend over to stand up here, but not me," Irma said with a hint of pride in her voice.

Meg smiled. "It is close up here."

Irma walked to a stack of paintings leaning against a wall and grabbed the tallest one from the back of the stack. She pulled it out and stood behind it so Meg could get a good look.

It was a picture of a door whose frame was surrounded by royal blue morning glories. The plain wooden door was weather worn and sad, as if long forgotten by those who had crossed its threshold. Meg felt drawn to its loneliness.

"It's beautiful," Meg said.

"It's the door Colin Brinker made for the Christmas cottage," Irma said. "And it was painted by Molly Brinker."

"I've always wondered why they called it the Christmas cottage," Meg said.

"The miracle happened on Christmas."

"What miracle?"

"A terrible nor'easter blew in on Christmas Eve, the night they were married, and when they woke up the next morning, the cottage had been spared. There was no damage to it, and both Colin and Molly were as right as rain."

Irma brought it closer to Meg, and she touched its surface.

"It's painted on wood. It must be heavy."

"Not so much that the two of us couldn't get it downstairs." Irma smiled. "I want you to have it."

"Oh, I couldn't." Meg looked at the painting again. It had a sweet quality that she liked, but she couldn't imagine why Irma would want to *give* it to her.

"It's just sitting up here when it should be where it belongs. Molly would be so disappointed to think of it sitting in this dusty old attic."

"At least let me give you something for it."

"No, no, it's a house-warming gift. I won't hear another word about it. Now, help me get it downstairs."

4

Meg parked her car close to her front door and struggled to get the large painting out of the back of her SUV. Irma had shown strength beyond her years as they carried to the car, which was several yards away, and helped Meg get it inside.

In the sunlight, she got a good look at it. The gold leaf on the thick wooden frame was chipping away, as was some of the paint in the picture. She wondered if it would fit through the doorframe, but as she stood it by the door, she saw that there was plenty of room at the top. She smiled; the painting was of this door, and seeing the two of them side by side was strange. She didn't recall seeing morning glories when she bought the house, and decided she would plant some in the spring.

Meg went inside and looked around the living room. She moved the old TV stand to one side and placed the painting against the wall. Irma said Molly Brinker had painted it and seemed to talk about her as if she had known her personally. Maybe that's how the old woman felt about the artists whose works appeared in her gallery.

She spent the rest of the day sorting through her

clothes for her trip to California. She hadn't traveled in so long that she had no idea what she'd have to do once she got to the airport, or what sort of luggage to take with her. By six, she was starving, so she made some soup and ate it in front of the TV. She woke up at ten and realized she had fallen asleep on the sofa.

Gray clouds greeted Meg as she went outside the next morning. The wind was bitterly cold and the grass frozen. When she lived in Boston, she always took a morning walk, but there were sidewalks there. The rough terrain surrounding the cottage made the walk a chore rather than something she looked forward to at the start of her day.

When she returned to the cottage, she built a fire in the hearth, and went to the kitchen to have her breakfast. In the past, someone had added a six-foot extension to the original kitchen, which allowed her to have a small table with two chairs underneath the window facing the back yard. She loved watching the birds plowing the snow with their beaks in search of seeds.

Meg saw a cardinal perched on the branch of the massive holly bush and the sight reminded her of a Currier and Ives print her grandmother had hung in her upstairs hallway. All that was missing were the sounds of bells on a bob-tailed horse pulling a sleigh toward the old farmhouse and shouts of *Merry Christmas*.

She had planned to spend the day in front of the hearth with a good book, and even though she was going to California for the holiday, that bird had put her in a holiday mood and she felt like decorating her new home.

Maddie had kept the old family decorations at her house, and when she died, Meg had kept them. As she got up to put her dishes in the sink, though, something caught her eye. She looked at the spot on the wall where Angus O'Malley had placed his hands on Thanksgiving Day and her mouth went dry. Chalky pastel colors in various shades were appearing in patches. The formerly white wall now had hues of pink, dark yellow, and lavender on top and varying shades of gray and teal on the bottom. In between the two was a large dark brown blotch, and over that spot were smudges of white and gray.

Meg stared at the spot, which was changing as she watched, and dropped her coffee mug. The sound of it hitting the floor roused her and she was grateful it hadn't shattered. She took it to the sink, and then put her hand near the wall. As she gathered her courage, she touched it with her fingers; the colors didn't come off on her hand. Then she realized that the white smudges above the brown blotch were moving back and forth like a billowing sail.

Fear and fascination fought for dominance as she stared at the wall. The splotches and smudges were taking shape, but the hand of the artist remained invisible. She took a few steps to get a better look as she fought the urge to run from the room. Soon discernible images emerged; the hull of a three-masted ship, a dark gray and teal roiling sea, and the most beautiful sunset Meg had ever seen.

Meg shivered. She sat at the table and stared at the wall as more details emerged. Gulls dipping and soaring, a ship's wheel with a sturdy little man at the helm, and a tiny sailboat bobbing at the ship's side where a rope ladder awaited its passenger.

Meg's heart was pounding, and she feared she might be having a heart attack. She was too far from her cell phone, but she had to get to it, so she got up slowly. When she didn't keel over, she went to the living room and sat on the sofa next to her phone.

Meg waited for pain in her back, arms, or jaw to come, but felt nothing but a twinge of arthritis in her hip along with her pounding heart. It was most likely a panic attack, which she'd had a few times since losing Maddie, but each time it happened she thought she was going to die. It always reminded her how alone she was, how vulnerable, and then she would cry.

She thought about the wall and the painting. What was it doing there? Then she remembered Angus O'Malley running his hands over it and wondered if he had done something to create the image. When she was a kid, they made coloring books that had colors that were invisible until you added water to them. Then the colors would appear like magic. Maybe the heat from Angus' hands brought out the images.

"That's ridiculous," she said.

It had been days since he'd been there. She reminded herself that magic didn't exist. She needed normalcy, boring reality, but the image appearing out of nowhere was anything but normal. It shook her to her core, and made her reluctant to go into the kitchen for the rest of the morning.

As she sat on the sofa, she wracked her brain for anything she might have researched for her books that might explain what she had just seen, but she wrote romances, not paranormal mysteries. Her stories were grounded in reality and the only magic that occurred was between the couple's sheets. With a wary eye, she glanced at the bedroom and thought about the computer. Maybe it was time to face that blank monitor again.

She went to the computer and turned it on. After it booted, she opened her research files and looked through them, but all she could find were articles on proper Victorian etiquette, which included things like the silent language of the fan, but nothing to do with ghosts. She wasn't even sure what type of phenomenon she had experienced, so she wrote "pictures appearing on wall."

Meg found articles saying that some people had experienced oily stains appearing on walls, and others drawings, but they were often associated with hauntings. Since Meg didn't believe in such things and hadn't encountered any spirits, she dismissed the idea of ghosts completely.

She sat back in her chair and sighed. Many of the articles suggested hiring a psychic, but that idea just made her giggle. While she believed everyone was entitled to their opinion, Meg didn't believe in what she could only see as "ghostbusters," a purely fictional concept.

It was past noon and she thought she should get dressed. She took a shower and put on an old pair of jeans and a sweatshirt. After stalling for several minutes while she sorted through her dirty clothes, she finally got up the nerve to go to the kitchen.

The laundry room consisted of an all-in-one washer/dryer that had been installed on the wall on the other side of the kitchen. It used the same pipes as the bathroom. As she walked toward it with her laundry basket, she couldn't stop her eyes from glancing at the painting. The image was clearer now, and a tiny sailor was hanging on the rope ladder. The details were amazing, but it was the little figure climbing down the ladder that drew her attention and she watched as it moved downward.

"Holy crap," she said when she realized what was happening, and dropped the basket. She backed away, grabbed her coat, and went outside.

They sky had cleared and it looked beautiful. Nature acted as if there was nothing wrong. It was just another day, and Meg tried to center herself and calm her erratic emotions.

"Think rationally," she said. "What could cause something like that?"

Electricity. Yes, someone might have created a weird piece of art that worked on a timer set to go off once a year at Christmas.

"Oh, brother," she said. "Come on, Meg. Think."

She went to the side of the cottage where the image had appeared and looked at the aluminum siding. It looked no different than the other sides of the cottage, which was square but for that six-foot extension in back. The roof was gabled and the window shutters were black. Meg could find no line going into the wall and she hesitated before getting on her knees to check underneath for her arthritis had gotten worse with the cold. It didn't matter; she knew there was no electrical line. There had never been a line, and now she had to find some other way to explain what was happening in her kitchen.

5

Meg spent a restless afternoon and night, but Saturday arrived and the plumber would be coming to talk about her pipes. She had to go to the kitchen to make coffee and eat breakfast, so she avoided looking at the wall. She wondered if this thing, whatever it was that was creating this animated image, might be dangerous, but what would she do if it was? By the time she found out, she would be either dead or insane, and neither prospect brought her any comfort.

After cleaning the dishes, Meg went to the bedroom to shower and dress. She kept looking at the drains in the shower and began to feel like she was in a Stephen King novel. Here's Johnny! Meg shuddered and got out of the shower, dried off, and put on some warm clothes so she could go to town. She would wander around the shops until it was time for the plumber to arrive.

At noon, after walking up and down the sidewalk for two hours, she stopped at a small café that had had a lunch counter since Meg was a girl. She and Maddie spent a lot on sodas and French fries each summer, and now, she took the same seat she'd sat in then. She ordered a grilled cheese, soda, and fries. Much to her chagrin, they were not the same. The fries were limp, the cheese hard, and the soda flat, but while she was sitting there, Zack called and told her he was coming for Christmas.

"I was thinking about that snow," he said. "Ethan grew up in Mississippi and has never had a white Christmas, so we figured that since we'd abandoned you at Thanksgiving, why not come to you instead of making you come all the way out here?"

Her heart fell. She had been looking forward to getting away, especially now that she had some sort of manic invisible painter mucking up her kitchen wall. Still, it would be nice to have him there, and to give Ethan a white Christmas, but what would they say about her little sailor?

When she didn't answer, Zack continued. "It's okay with you if we come, right?"

"Yes, sure, of course."

"So, do we have to find a hotel room or will you let us sleep together on the pullout sofa?"

She smiled. "I don't know. You're not married."

"That never stopped one of your bodice ripping heroines from throwing herself at some long-haired alpha male. Come to think of it, it wouldn't have stopped me, either."

"All right, make fun, but people love my stories *and* my heroines, who, by the way, are intelligent and courageous."

"Yeah, yeah, whatever. So, what do you say, Meg? Can we come for Christmas?"

"Of course you can come, *and* you can stay with me."

She loved hearing his voice and couldn't wait to see Zack. He was as practical as she, but he read a lot of science fiction and might be able to come up with some explanation for the weird goings-on in her kitchen. He also knew technology. Yes, Zack might know exactly what was going on.

The plumber arrived as promised and saw the painting on the wall. While he was there, though, it didn't move, or change in any way. Meg had hoped it would so he could give her some idea what might have caused it, but he merely looked at it and grunted.

She thought of the way Angus had touched the wall and asked the plumber if there were any pipes in that wall.

"Naw," he said. "They run from this here sink to the bathroom." He pointed to the right. "That way."

"And can you tell me if there's any other way to keep the pipes from bursting until we can get them wrapped?"

He shook his head, and added wrapping to the estimate, which was already way over her budget. She'd have to continue her search for someone she could afford. In the meantime, she now had a good reason to get the house decorated and turn her home into a festive homage to Santa Claus.

Meg glanced at the wall as she filled the glass pot from the coffeemaker. The tiny sailboat was away from the ship now, and the tiny sailor was steering the boat through choppy seas, cutting a swath in the painted sea, as he headed in the direction of her sink. For a moment, she thought the little guy might pop up out of her drain, and she looked at it and pulled her the pot away.

"I'm getting a garbage disposal," she said. "Poke your head out of my drain and you'll regret it."

For reasons she failed to understand, she had stopped being afraid of the painting and had begun to look forward to seeing its progress. Seeing the details appear was fascinating, and she wondered if it would stop when Zack arrived as it had when the plumber was there.

"But that would mean you truly are crazy," she said.

As her coffee brewed, she checked her emails on her phone and looked out the window. When the coffeemaker sputtered, she got up and poured a cup, and then went back to the table. When she looked up at the wall, the sailboat had traveled at least five inches from the ship. Just the quarter of the ship remained as the sailboat sailed away, and it occurred to her that while she had thought the subject of the artwork was the grand three-masted ship, it was instead the tiny sailboat and the three-inch sailor at its helm.

Meg watched the painting while she ate her dinner that night. Morbid curiosity consumed her as the boat made its way across the wall. Progress was slow and steady, and she still feared finding the little man waltzing across her table any day now, but it took her mind off other things, giving her respite from her sadness, and sometimes she felt grateful for the odd distraction.

The sailboat was now alone on the high seas, and the focus zoomed in on the man rowing. Meg got up and went to the wall to get a closer look. He had a dark beard, wore a pea coat and cap, and his expression was hard as if he had to concentrate all his might on holding the tiller.

She backed away and folded her arms across her chest.

"I am losing my mind," she said.

Meg left her dishes on the table and went to the living room where the decorations sat on the floor in a box. She'd have to get a small tree, but not until it was closer to Christmas or it would dry out and the floor would be covered in pine needles. Her mind kept going back to the wall and the sailor. She needed a distraction from her distraction, so she went to her room to play video games on the computer.

After trying to focus on solitaire and failing miserably, she decided to look up Molly Brinker, née Barton. Someone had created a Wikepedia page about her and it mentioned Molly's husband,

Colin Brinker, a ship's captain who'd been lost at sea crossing the Bermuda Triangle. There was no picture of Captain Brinker, but Molly had been captured on canvas and she was a rather pretty girl with dark hair and soulful eyes.

The article mentioned her career as a writer and how she'd lived in the cottage Colin built for her until 1878. Meg was disappointed by the lack of information and shut the laptop in dismay, and then reopened it when she got an idea.

Meg began to search for local historians who might know more about Molly and this cottage. She wanted to know if Molly had dabbled in magic, or if she'd had a reputation as a witch. She felt foolish even thinking it, but at this point, Meg was willing to hear any explanation for what was happening in her kitchen.

Meg had always believed in the rational explanation for the Salem witches – that the girls who'd been "possessed" were probably victims of infected rye, which can cause hallucinations. Seeking information that would confirm Molly was a witch would go against everything she believed in, but so did the evidence on her wall.

Meg sat back and sighed. Maddie had been the great romantic in the family, the one who believed in fairy tales, and her childlike belief in spiritual things had drawn people to her. But Meg was more serious. She'd had trouble making friends, preferring the company of her siblings, and when she started writing, it became her refuge. You could control the people you wrote about and you always knew what they were going to do.

But they were also invisible, these characters she brought to life on a page, and right now she wished she had a living, breathing person to sleep in the house with her after she turned off the lights.

There it was again, that awful, lonely ache that wouldn't go away. At this stage of her life, she wanted a good man with whom she could have lively conversations, and perhaps some nookie under the covers.

There had been men in her past who'd tried to get past the walls she so loved, but they had grown weary of her need to have things her way, and she would tell herself after they left that it was just as well, that she didn't need them. Now, there were fewer opportunities, and her lack of companionship culminated in a belief that she was truly unlovable.

As long as her siblings were around, she could pretend she wasn't alone. Now she wondered if her mind was leaving her, too.

Meg stretched and turned off the computer. It was time to go to bed to try and get some sleep, but she couldn't resist one more peek at the kitchen wall. The little sailboat was on calmer seas and the little sailor was taking a nap.

6

Meg watched the tiny sailboat's progress for two weeks as it traversed the painted sea. She watched the sail billow in the wind and saw gulls fly by, taunting the sailor for a piece of bread, and then flying out of the picture.

She was watching the sailor guiding the boat past a large rock when Zack called and told her they would be arriving on the twenty-third.

"Just make that fudge I like," he said. "We're gonna take you out to dinner."

Meg had been cleaning and getting things ready and she was confident that she hadn't forgotten anything. They had agreed not to give presents this year, and she hoped Zack would honor that decision. She made cookies and fudge, and stored them in Ziplock containers so he could take some home.

Another week passed, and Zack was due to arrive in a few days. Meg got up that morning and went to the bathroom. She rarely looked at her face first thing in the morning and avoided the mirror over the sink by keeping her eyes down while she washed her hands and brushed her teeth, but this day she did so without thinking.

At sixty-two, Meg had retained much of her natural hair color, with a few strands of gray that you could barely see, so when she saw her reflection, the first thing she noticed was that her hair looked different. All the familiar gray strands were gone. She mussed her hair with her hands, trying to make them appear, but found none.

Then she focused on her face. The laugh lines had softened, and the bags under her eyes weren't as noticeable. The skin under her neck looked tighter, and she thought about the expensive lotion she'd been persuaded to buy while walking through Macy's one afternoon. Meg HAD followed the saleswoman's instructions to a tee, but these results were off the charts!

"I could do a commercial for this stuff."

After she showered, Meg passed the old box of decorations in the living room for the hundredth time and thought it was time to get a tree. After she drank her coffee and had a piece of toast, she sat on the sofa and looked through the box.

As Meg held them up one by one, each childish school project or Hallmark annual ornament, or "special" glass bulb, would cause her to tear up. She remembered these decorations on her parents' tree, and the way they had all come to the big house in Springfield every year. Maddie and she had cleaned that house after her mother died because Eddie was sick and couldn't help them. The loneliness was threatening to consume her, so she shut the box and went to get her coat. A walk would do her good.

As Meg looked around the yard, she made a list in her head of all the things she'd have to do before Zack's arrival. Besides the tree, she'd have to buy and hang new strings of lights, which she would get in the Hyannis Target.

Meg went back to the kitchen sink to finish the dishes and felt her jeans slipping down her hips. While ordinarily she would have been thrilled by this, she hadn't done anything to lose weight, and at her age, sudden weight loss could be a sign of some dreaded disease. As the jeans slipped down her legs, Meg pulled them up and held them until she found a belt in her drawer and put it on, and then she added jeans to her shopping list.

7

Meg cut another hole in the belt before leaving the house later that afternoon. She cinched it tightly and then put on her coat. The sleeves were too long and the hem was almost to her knees. She had to go to find a tree and do her shopping, so she tried to ignore what was happening to her body and got into the SUV.

Meg had to adjust the seat on the car so she could reach the pedals, but soon she was on her way to find the perfect Christmas tree. It had to be on the small side so it would fit in her living room, and so she went to a place she'd found online that had trees you could plant after the holiday, which she hoped would be smaller.

The nursery was off the main road near Brewster. It had a long, dirt road that led to a greenhouse bearing a sign that read, "Hooper's Landscaping." Meg parked near the building and got out of her car, and as she did, she felt her jeans shift. When she began to walk, the jeans felt loose, and she stopped to check them, making sure the belt was still in place. It was, but there was a wider gap between her stomach and the pants, so she kept her hand on the waist.

Hooper's did have a nice assortment of trees, both potted and cut, and the smell was wonderful. Pine and cinnamon filled the air, and an older woman dressed as Mrs. Claus was offering hot apple cider at the checkout counter. Mr. Hooper was Santa Claus, and Meg noticed that he didn't need a pillow to fatten him up for the role. He smiled when he saw her and came to greet her with his hand extended.

"Merry Christmas," he said in a booming voice that reverberated off the walls. The echo drowned out the carols being piped in over a loudspeaker.

"Hello, Santa," Meg said. "I like your suit."

"Mrs. Claus takes good care of me." He looked at his plump wife and winked, then looked at Meg. "So, where do you come from?"

"Port Revere."

"Ah, yes. I was to Port Revere once and it's a lovely town. It's a bit of a drive though."

"I came here hoping you would have smaller trees. My living room is just about six feet and I want a star on my tree."

"No worries. Donner will have just what you're looking for."

Meg followed Santa to the back of the greenhouse where she saw a brown and tan dappled miniature horse in a pen. A sign edged in candy cane colors read "Donner."

"Hey, Donner, old pal, do we have a tree for the nice lady?"

That was the horse's cue, and he nodded his head

and stamped his little hoof.

"He's adorable," Meg said.

"He's almost twenty years old. Got him the first year we opened the greenhouse to sell trees at Christmas and he's been my best salesman."

The mini went back to munching on hay as Santa led her to a row of freshly cut trees.

"I have a nice four-footer I'd like to show you. Good tree. I chopped it down myself just yesterday."

Meg smiled. She wondered if he said this about every tree in the place. He stopped in front of an upright stack of trees and pulled one out to show her.

"This is it. See how nice the boughs fall." It was a nice, full tree that came to the top of Santa's chest. "It's a cut tree. You weren't lookin' for a potted tree, were you? I forgot to ask."

"No, no, just a small tree that doesn't look scraggly."

"Well, this is one proud little tree, don't ya think?"

"I agree."

"Well, then, let's take 'er on over to Mrs. Claus and have us some apple cider."

"Wait," she said. "How much is it?"

"This here is a Fraser fir. It's one of the finest you can buy."

"And it costs?"

"Well, since you're such a nice lady and all, I can't charge you more than a ten spot a foot for 'er."

"Forty dollars." He nodded. "The last time I

bought one, it was twenty-five, and I thought that was a lot."

"This here is a Fraser fir. You ask anybody and they'll tell you what a grand tree it is."

"I'm sure it's a great tree, but I still think that's a lot for a small tree."

"Why, people in Boston are paying fifteen dollar a foot. I've been getting more and more customers comin' in every weekend."

Santa was giving her the old hard sell, and she did want a nice tree for Zack and Ethan.

"I'll tell you what," he said. "I'll throw in a box of tinsel free for nothing."

"Oh, well, you've worn me down. I'll take it."

Santa grinned and carried the tree to the checkout counter. He then grabbed a box of tinsel off a shelf near the cash register and Mrs. Claus beamed.

"Give this to the little lady free of charge, Mama."

"He drives a hard bargain," Meg said.

"He has a lot of reindeer to feed," Mrs. Claus said with a chuckle.

"And one horse."

"Oh, Donner is a love, isn't he?"

"He has a beautiful coat," Meg said.

"The kids love him. I keep carrots back here for them to feed him. So, will this be all?"

"Yes."

Mrs. Claus rang her items and then called to Santa to take the tree to Meg's car. He tied it to the roof and waved as she drove away.

"Merry Christmas!" he cried.

"And to all a good night," she said softly.

Meg was able to get the tree into the house and stand it in the corner next to the bay window. As she struggled to get it through the door, her jeans shifted again, and went to her hips.

What the hell is going on with these jeans? she thought.

After setting the tree against the wall, Meg went to the bedroom and looked into the mirror. Her jeans were at least two sizes too big, and she went to the dresser to find a pair of sweatpants with a string tie. When she took off her jeans, she looked at her body in the mirror and saw that it, like her face, looked different, as if she'd had a body lift. She also noticed that the bags under her eyes were smaller.

Before leaving the house again, Meg went to the kitchen to look at the wall. The little boat was at another point on the wall. Did the painting have anything to do with her changing appearance? Thoughts of Molly Brinker as a sorceress flitted through her mind again, but she didn't have time to wonder if the cottage was possessed. She had to get the rest of her shopping done.

She looked down at the sweatpants and decided to go to Target first to get a new pair of jeans and the other things on her list. She might as well have fun with her new body in case it didn't last. She drove to Hyannis, went straight to the women's department, and noticed that some of the men she passed looked at her a bit longer than necessary. It made her feel good for it had been a long time since she'd garnered such looks.

Her steps were lighter and her mood elevated as she approached the stand full of folded jeans. She picked a pair that was two sizes smaller than she'd worn before, and then another three sizes smaller just in case she continued to shrink.

A young woman straightening the shelves smiled at her and asked her if she needed any help. Meg smiled in return and said no, but the girl's attention irritated her. When she'd shopped for clothes before, she was seldom asked if she needed help, as salespeople were more interested in pursuing younger clientele. They were going to spend more money than a sixty-something who didn't feel the need to impress anyone anymore.

Meg picked out a pair of jeans and went to the mirror to hold them against her, and looked at her face, too. The bags under her eyes were gone now, and the roses in her cheeks brighter. It was odd to be looking at someone she hadn't seen in thirty years staring back at her. Did she even know this girl?

Meg had nothing in common with her reflection, and was surprised by her reaction to the changes. She always thought it would be fun to turn back time for a day or two, to visit her old self and tell her to enjoy life more, but now that it was happening, she was confused and frightened. All the changes she'd gone through as she'd grown into the woman she'd become were flowing through Meg's mind as if she had to decide which to keep and which to discard. Letting go of even one would change her, and she didn't know if it would be for better or worse.

Damn it, Meg, why can't you just follow your own advice and enjoy this? she thought. "Because it has to end."

"Did you say something?" the salesgirl asked.

"Just talking to myself," Meg said.

"Oh, I do that all the time," the young woman said. She smiled. She was still ignorant of the things life would throw at her, and Meg envied her innocence.

She wished she could share what was happening with Maddie. She was always going on about her thighs, or her stomach, and she would have been tickled by the idea of losing two sizes in one day. The full weight of Meg's loneliness fell on her like a concrete block, so she dropped the jeans and left the store. She could barely contain the tears before getting into her car and slamming the door shut. The deep well of self-pity she'd suppressed while watching the little sailor and focusing on Zack's visit bubbled forth, causing her to sob uncontrollably.

A misspent life. The phrase kept looping in her mind along with an overwhelming sense of regret. She'd done nothing she'd wanted to when she was a girl. She'd abandoned her dreams as others told her they were foolish and unattainable to someone like her, someone whose capacity for learning was average at best, and who never seemed to finish anything she started.

Now anger came, a rage so big and out of control she dare not start the car or she might ram it into the car in front of her until the vehicle was unrecognizable.

As her heart rate slowed and her anger dissipated, Meg's breathing normalized and she felt the tension leave her shoulders. She closed her eyes and exhaled loudly. She stayed that way for fifteen minutes and then went back to the store to buy the jeans.

Meg went down the Christmas aisle, a mass of disarray, and was able to find a tree stand and strings of lights. After she paid for her items, Meg drove home and took them inside. The house was dark and she switched on the light before heading to the kitchen for something to eat. The little sailor was again fighting a churning sea and the wind blew hard against him. She marveled that his cap remained in place, and wondered at her own acceptance of the strange situation, then Meg realized that having him here meant that she was not alone.

8

As she placed the old family ornaments on the tree, Meg thought about growing up with Maddie and Eddie, each fighting to place his or her ornament on the same branch, the best branch, and each nearly knocking the poor tree down. They had fought a lot then, but when they reached adulthood, they were friends, and they had each other's backs.

Meg put one of Eddie's ornaments near the center of the tree. He had cut the construction paper into the shape of a star and had added a black and white photo of him in his pajamas near a Christmas tree in the center that had been cut into a star, too. Some sparkles enhanced the edges, and the back of it read, "Eddie, 1952."

It had been made before Meg was born, but Maddie was a baby. Maddie's ornament was plaster with a painted Santa on it rendered in childish strokes and dated "1959." Meg had one, too, which meant they had to have done it in one of the ceramic classes her mother made them attend.

After getting the annual Hallmark ones in place, she stepped back to admire her work. It looked good, and she was happy. She thought her siblings would be proud to see her tree and the places of honor their ornaments held.

Meg went on the computer and checked her email. Zack had sent her his itinerary, and this reminded her she had to put sheets on the pullout sofa and make the fudge because he'd asked her to.

A trip to the grocery store, Meg was exhausted, but she still had a lot to do. She put the sheets on the pullout, dusted, vacuumed, shoved her clothes aside and added hangers to the rack in the armoire. After she was satisfied with the room, she cleaned the living room and bathroom.

Her new jeans fit well, but she already felt them getting looser. Meg hoped this wasn't some sort of curse like the one in Stephen King's *Thinner*, but she didn't recall that man growing younger, too. Her face was now wrinkle-free, and her hair had taken on a luster it hadn't had since she was a teenager, but the one thing she loved more than anything else was the lack of pain in her joints. She had a spring in her step and she slept well, too.

Meg opened the can of condensed milk and poured it into a large microwave bowl. She added 18 oz. of semi-sweet chocolate chips and a teaspoon of vanilla, and then stuck the bowl in the microwave for three minutes and greased a square pan. When the timer went off, Meg took the bowl out of the microwave, stirred it to make sure all the chips were melted, and then poured the concoction into the greased pan. As she was pouring, Meg thought about Zack and froze.

What will he think when he sees me? How will I explain this?

She could tell him she'd had some work done, but she'd seen older women after surgery and while they looked younger, they didn't look as they had when they were eighteen. No surgeon on Earth could do that. She decided to confess to a small lift and let it go, even if he pressed her.

That night, she slept well again, but woke up in the middle of the night thinking about Zack. He would press her about her physical changes, and he could be like a dog with a bone when confronted by a mystery. She'd seen him do it since he was a boy. If it were only her face that had changed, he might let it go, but she was two sizes smaller and felt shorter, and that would spark an investigation on his part.

The following day, as the hours passed and Zack's plane was due to land, Meg paced the floor. When she looked at herself in the mirror, she looked even younger than she had the day before. She went back and forth on whether to tell him the truth, but what was the truth, that the cottage was enchanted?

She tried playing video games as she waited for his phone call telling her they were on their way, but she couldn't sit still. She put on her coat and went for a short walk, but as she walked down the hill, her mind kept going around what she would say to Zack. Meg had always thought too much, and she'd tried to develop the habit of stopping thoughts before they went over a cliff of unreality, but now that something fantastical had happened to her, it was hard to stop them.

"Stop it," she said. "Just tell him you had a lift."

She returned to the house and went to the kitchen to make some tea. As Meg waited for the kettle to boil, she looked at the wall. The little boat was nearing a dock, and as she studied the painting, she saw a familiar building nearby – the old lighthouse. The lighthouse itself had been destroyed in a hurricane years ago, but in the painting, it was still there, its red and white strips as bright as the day they were painted, all set to greet the little sailor when he tied his sailboat to the dock.

9

Zack and Ethan arrived a couple of hours later, and the little boat had reached its destination. Meg thought of covering it with a sheet, but that would only draw their attention to it. Why hadn't she tried to paint over it while she had the chance? Probably because she knew it wouldn't work.

Meg answered the door, embraced them both, and watched as their expressions changed from joy to shock.

"My God, Meg," Zack said. "You look so… different."

"You really do," Ethan said.

She held back on the torrent of words threatening to spill out of her mouth and smiled, and then bit her lower lip.

"Really, Meg," Zack said. "What happened to you?"

"Nothing," Meg said. "Would anyone like some coffee?"

While she went to the kitchen, Zack looked at Ethan with wide eyes.

"Have you ever seen anything like that?" Ethan shook his head. "She looks like a teenager."

"I'd like the name of her doctor," Ethan said, running his fingers along the lines under his eyes.

"No shit." Zack looked at the tree. "Why won't she talk about it?"

Ethan shrugged. "I wouldn't push her."

"Yeah, but it's gonna kill me until I find out."

Meg brought a tray with a carafe, three mugs, sugar, and milk and put it on the end table next to the sofa.

"Ethan?" He shook his head. "Zack?"

"I'll have some."

"The tree looks good," Ethan said.

"Thanks. I bought it in Brewster from Santa Claus."

Meg smiled, and they did, too, but Zack couldn't stop staring at her. He crossed one leg over the other and his foot started shaking.

"So," he said. "We thought we'd hit some of the shops in town while we're here."

"That's a good idea," she said as she poured his coffee. "What do you take in this?"

"Sugar." His foot was moving faster until he put it down and stood up. "Who are you?"

She put the mug down and looked at him. "I'm your Aunt Meg."

"No, you're not. I don't know who you are, but there's no way you can be my Aunt Meg."

"I swear to you, Zack, I am Meg."

"Meg is sixty-two years old!"

"I know, and I know I look younger…."

"Younger! You're a freaking zygote, for God's

sake!"

"Zack," Ethan said.

"Why would I tell you I'm Meg when I'm not?"

"I don't know. Maybe you ran away from home. Maybe you killed Meg and are living here because you didn't think anyone would find out."

"It is weird," Ethan said.

"Don't you think I know it's weird?" she asked.

Zack was taking his phone out of his pocket. "I'm calling the police."

"What?" She went to him and put her hand on his arm. "Please, Zack, don't do that."

"Something happened to my aunt and I'm gonna find out what."

"Nothing has happened, well, not anything illegal."

She looked up at him, and something in her eyes stopped him from dialing.

"If you're my Aunt Meg, what did you give me for my fourteenth birthday?"

"A pair of parachute pants like M.C. Hammer's."

Zack looked confused, but strengthened his resolve and stared into her eyes.

"What branch of the service was my Uncle Eddie in?"

"The Air Force. He didn't go to Vietnam. He spent his whole tour in New Mexico."

Now Zack was confused. She had the right answers.

"When's my mom's birthday?"

"December 16th."

Zack backed away. He didn't know how she knew, but he was willing to hear what she had to say in the way of an explanation.

"If you're Meg, why do you look like this?"

Now Meg went to the sofa and sat. "I don't know. It started happening a few days ago." She looked at him. "And that's not all that's been happening." She got up and went to the kitchen. "Come here."

Ethan got up and followed Zack to the kitchen. They looked at Meg, and then at the chalky drawing on the wall.

"I don't remember that being there," Zack said.

Ethan noticed the details, which were extraordinary for a chalk drawing.

"It's amazing," he said.

"Did you do this?" Zack asked.

"No. It appeared sometime after Thanksgiving. It...changes every day."

"What do you mean it changes?" Ethan asked.

"I mean it changes, it's different every time I look at it."

Zack looked at the lighthouse. "Wasn't there a lighthouse *here* a long time ago?"

"Yes, and it was near the dock, just like in the picture."

They were all quiet for a long time, and then Zack sighed.

"Okay, so it's weird, so what do we do about it?"

Meg and Ethan exchanged glances. She looked at the picture and noticed that the little sailor was standing on the dock.

"He was on the sailboat yesterday," she said.

"I wonder who he is," Ethan said.

"I think I know," she said, "but I have no way of knowing for sure."

"Who?" Zack said.

"A sea captain who disappeared in 1855."

"Oh, well, then it all makes sense." Zack shook his head.

"Zack," Ethan said.

"Sorry," Zack said. He looked at Meg. "So why is he on your wall?"

"His name was Colin Brinker. He built this cottage for the woman he loved. People always said the cottage was enchanted because when he made it, he sealed it with love."

"Oh, brother," Zack said.

"But that doesn't explain your appearance," Ethan said. "Why are you getting younger?"

Meg looked as if she was about to cry, and Zack felt bad about yelling at her.

"Hey, I've got an idea," he said. "Why don't we get out of here for a while? We can go into town and look around."

Now Meg looked relieved. "Are you sure you're not too tired?"

"No, not at all," Zack said and then he looked at Ethan, who shook his head, too.

"Okay," she said. "Let's go."

They drove to town in the SUV the boys had rented at the airport. The town was full of last-minute shoppers and Meg directed Zack to the public parking lot, but they still had to circle around before finding a spot.

The music that day was traditional carols, and as they walked down the sidewalk, they looked into the shop windows where happy shopkeepers helped last-minute customers. Now and then, Ethan or Zack would want to stop and go inside, but Meg stayed on the sidewalk to listen to the music and smell the fresh air.

As they neared the gallery, Meg thought about the painting by Molly Brinker. Ethan suggested they stop and see if there were any nautical paintings by local artists, and Meg followed them inside this time because she wanted to see Irma and ask if she knew anything about Colin Brinker. A young woman was helping a customer when they walked in but Irma was nowhere in sight.

Ethan and Zack looked at paintings while Meg waited at the counter, which held an old-fashioned register and a small statue of a black Lab. The inscription at the base of the statue said "Barney." She remembered the old black Lab Angus brought with him and wondered if this dog was one of his ancestors.

Her eyes then wandered to the wall behind the counter. Photographs set at different levels filled the wall, and in the center was a photo of an old man in front of a truck. A black dog sat in the truck, and she saw the top of a capital "A" painted on the truck's door.

"Angus O'Malley."

She could hear his voice. The old plumber appeared once, touched her wall, and had never returned. He was an odd duck, and now she wondered if he might be related to Irma. Upon closer inspection, though, she noticed the old-fashioned scalloped edges on the black and white photograph, which was yellowed with age.

The young woman came behind the counter to get something and Meg touched her arm.

"Excuse me," she said. "Is that Angus O'Malley?"

The young woman smiled. "Yes it is. He's one of my ancestors. His claim to fame was that he'd installed the first bathroom in the United States right up there in that cottage on the hill."

Meg felt her cheeks redden. "When was that?"

"Geez, I'm not sure, but sometime in the 1800's."

Now the color drained from her cheeks as she saw another photograph on the wall.

"And that lady," she said pointing to it, "Is that Irma?"

"Yes, wow, you sure know a lot about my relatives. She was Angus' daughter."

"And when was that taken?" Meg asked, her voice quivering.

"That was in the twenties. She was my mother's great-great-grandmother."

"But that can't be," Meg said softly. "She gave me tea, and she had petit fours, and I ate them."

"I'm sorry," the young woman said.

Meg looked pale. "She was here. She gave me a painting. We sat at that table in back and *we had tea*!"

Meg went to the back of the store with the young woman following close behind.

"Miss, are you all right?"

When they got to the back of the store, Meg stopped dead in her tracks. The space near the window now held an L-shaped sofa and a coffee table.

"But it was here. I know it was here."

"What was here?" The young woman looked concerned. "My mom put this couch here when she ran the gallery."

"But there was a table and chairs right there."

"I don't remember a table and chairs," the young woman said. "Just this couch."

Zack came to Meg's side.

"What's wrong?" he asked.

"She thinks she saw a table and chairs here, and had tea with my late grandmother."

"I'm sure she must mistaken," he said, and put his arm around Meg's shoulders. "I'm tired, Meg. What do you say we go home?"

"I did see her here," Meg kept saying. "She was here, and Angus O'Malley came to my house to check my pipes."

As they drove home, Zack and Ethan kept exchanging glances. Meg was upset and kept babbling about Angus and Irma. They worried that they might have to take her to the hospital, but what would they tell them, that Zack's sixty-two-year-old aunt was regressing physically and was delusional to boot?

When they walked inside the house, Meg stopped in front of the painting of the cottage door.

"Irma gave me this painting," she said.

"I was going to ask you about that," Zack said, "but then we got all caught up in figuring out who you were and all."

"It's unusual," Ethan said.

"It was painted by Molly Brinker," she said.

"Who the hell is Molly Brinker?" Zack asked.

"The owner of this house. Her husband built it for her."

"She was an obscure 19th century author who used a male pseudonym," Ethan said.

"How the hell do you know that?" Zack asked.

"She was one of the authors I studied for my thesis. She went mad before she died and ended up in an institution. I'd forgotten she was married to *Colin* Brinker."

"No," Meg said, her eyes wide in disbelief. "She couldn't have."

Ethan nodded. "She kept talking about her husband and how he was coming home."

They all thought of the picture on the kitchen wall.

"You don't think…" Zack said.

They all walked to the kitchen and looked at the wall. The little sailor was standing on the dock with a pipe in his hand. A stream of smoke rose from the picture, and they all took a step back.

"I thought I smelled cherry tobacco," Ethan said. "My uncle favored it. He'd smoke it in a corn cob pipe."

"How big was he?" Zack asked.

"He was life-size."

They stared at the picture until the sun went down and the room became dark. Meg switched on the light and looked at the stove.

"Is anyone hungry?"

"Why don't I cook?" Ethan said.

"He really likes to cook," Zack said.

"I would love that." Meg opened a cabinet and showed him where the pots and pans were.

Before they left Ethan alone, they took one more look at the painting. The little sailor was tapping his pipe against his foot, and then he looked at them. On impulse, Zack waved at him, and the little sailor waved back.

10

Zack and Meg were watching the news, and the aroma of Ethan's dinner was making them hungry.

"I hope it's done soon," Zack said. "I'm starving."

"It does smell good."

He looked at her and smiled. "So, tell me the truth. Did you draw that picture?"

Meg shook her head. "I swear to you it just appeared one day."

Zack stared at the TV.

"And you started to change right after Thanksgiving. Was that before or after you had tea with that girl's dead grandmother?"

"That's mean, Zack, and you were never mean to me."

"I have to ask, Meg. I'm trying to figure out what's happened to you."

"Well, if you do, will you please tell me?"

Meg got up and went to the bedroom, shut the door, and sat on the bed. She should have told him to stay home, or gone to California like she'd wanted to, but now it was too late. She got up and opened the bedroom door. Zack was still sitting on the sofa.

"I'm sorry," Meg said.

"No, I'm the one who's sorry. I shouldn't kid you about this."

Meg sat beside him and laid her head back. "At first there was a three-masted ship, with a small sailboat beside it, and the sailor was on a rope ladder. After a while, the little boat sailed away from the big ship, and he was alone on the water. Now he's on the dock in Port Revere, and I keep expecting him to pop up out of my drain."

Zack chuckled. "And he can see us."

"I don't know what to do," she said. "It's been one weird thing after another. I just wanted a quiet place to do my writing."

Zack put his hand on her hand. "It's a great cottage, Meg, but you might want to consider moving to a nice quiet cottage in California, or Maine."

"I put everything into this, Zack." She looked him in the eye. "It was vacant for forty years until I came along."

"Oh."

"Yeah, oh. It's not gonna be that easy to sell, and besides, I don't want to sell it. I just want the ghosts or the magic or whatever is going on here to stop."

"Yeah, I agree. It's freaking me out, too."

"So, what do you think is going on? Why would that girl's dead relatives come to me instead of her?"

"I have no idea." He put his head back. "You're a writer. What reason would a ghost have to visit someone?"

"This is like a paranormal fantasy, not the

fantasy I write about the lasting love between a man and a woman."

Meg got up and went to the bay window.

"So you think lasting love is a fantasy?"

"Absolutely." She looked at him. "The only reason those 18th century marriages lasted as long as they did was because they were arranged. Add a financial component, and women's lack of rights, and you have a lasting union."

"God, Meg, I had no idea you were so cynical."

"I'm just realistic."

"Then I must be a hopeless romantic because I believe you can love someone your whole life."

She smiled and looked at him.

"You're really happy with Ethan, aren't you?"

"More than I'd ever hoped to be."

"Then maybe you'll prove me wrong."

Zack caught a whiff of dinner.

"Ethan, when are we eating?" he shouted.

"Soon."

Zack sat forward. "I found a B&B when I was looking for a hotel before I knew you wanted us to stay here. Maybe we should consider going there."

"Who? You and Ethan?"

"No, all of us."

Meg came and sat beside him.

"No, not me. I won't let them, whoever they are, drive me out of my home."

Zack put his arm around her. She felt so small.

"Okay, then I guess we'll stay here and protect you. We can handle anything they can throw at us."

Meg put her head back on his shoulder and they sat that way for a long time until Ethan called them to the table. Zack brought a chair from the bedroom so they could all sit. She tried to focus on Zack and Ethan, but her eye caught some movement, which made her look at the wall. The little sailor was leaving the dock now and was on his way toward town.

11

Ethan was the first one up the next morning and Meg smiled when she smelled coffee brewing. She looked out the bedroom window at the gray sky and sighed. She sat up and saw more snow on the ground and knew it would probably snow again before nightfall.

Meg got out of bed and put on her slippers and robe before going to the bathroom.

"Good morning," she said to Ethan's back as he stood at the stove. He turned and smiled. "I see Zack is still asleep."

"He's not a morning person," Ethan said with a winsome smile. "It works for us. I get to do what I want in the morning, and he gets to do what he wants after I go to bed."

Meg went to the bathroom and then poured herself a cup of coffee.

"I could get used to this," she said.

Meg sat at the table and Ethan put some food on a plate and brought it to her.

"Oh, wow," she said. "You made this out of stuff from my fridge?"

"Biscuits and gravy, ham, and grits just like

grandma used to make."

"Where did you get the ham and grits?"

"I ran to the store."

Meg usually had a piece of toast for breakfast, but this was too good to pass up. Besides, she was starving, like she had been when she was a kid. The biscuits were light and flaky, and the gravy smooth. Ethan definitely knew his way around a kitchen.

Ethan kept glancing at her and she knew she must have changed again.

"Zack and I were talking last night and we thought we'd take a ride to Brinker today."

"Brinker?"

He nodded his head. "We stayed up and did some research on Colin Brinker. The town was named for his father who was the mayor there."

"I looked for him and couldn't find a thing."

"Zack is very good with a computer. He knows how to find stuff. Anyway, we thought we'd go check out the town. You game?"

"Sure."

She finished eating and got dressed, and then found Zack at the table when she came back to the kitchen. He looked tired and held onto his coffee mug for dear life.

"Hi, Zack," she said.

He grunted and held his head with his hand. Ethan rolled his eyes and finished washing the dishes.

"I would have done that," she said, but she was glad he'd done them. It was nice to be taken care of once in a while, especially by someone who knew what you needed before you did.

She sat at the table, clasped her hands in front of her, and kept her eyes on Zack. She saw Maddie in him, and for a second, she almost started to cry. A wave of gratitude for his presence washed over her and she got up and kissed his forehead.

"I really miss your mother," she said.

"I do, too." He looked at her with one eye. "You look younger."

She put her thumb in her waistband and pulled. "And these are bigger."

Grief was an odd emotion. It blindsided you when you least expected, and then would disappear for stretches of time without explanation. Seeing Zack renewed her sadness. She put her cheek next to Zack's and hugged his neck.

"I love you," she said.

He smiled. "I love you, too, Meg."

"A Hallmark moment," Ethan said.

"Oh, shut up," Zack said.

He balled up a paper napkin and threw it at Ethan, who ducked, and the napkin bounced off the wall behind him, hitting the little sailor, who jumped out of the way.

"Did you see that?" Zack asked.

"See what?"

"The little dude jumped out of the way when I threw the napkin."

Ethan wouldn't look at the wall, and Meg hadn't been looking at it when it happened.

"He *does* see us," Zack said.

"I think you're seeing things," Ethan said.

"You're just afraid of him."

"Not afraid, just skeptical."

"Then why won't you look at the picture?"

Ethan put the dishtowel down and leaned with his hands on the sink.

"Maybe it's just the way the light hits it."

"Ethan," Meg said. "We saw him smoking last night. You said you smelled cherry tobacco."

"There has to be some logical explanation."

Zack kept looking at the wall, but the sailor was still.

"He seems to know where he's going." Zack looked at Meg. "I think we should buy a bottle of wine when we're in town today."

"I could use a glass of wine," Meg said.

"Anything that will get you to stop talking about that sailor," Ethan said.

After Zack got dressed, they rode to Brinker. The town was similar to Port Revere – a main street with shops on each side, and a rotary in the center of town, only this rotary didn't have a Christmas tree, it had a bronze statue of a tall man.

They found an artisanal wine shop and bought two bottles, and then wandered down the sidewalk until they were near the statue.

"I'm gonna go over there and find out who he was," Zack said.

He ran across the street and read the placard. He turned to them with a broad smile and waved them over.

"Colin Brinker, son of Eustis Brinker, lost at sea in 1855."

"It's him," Meg said.

"And he was one big dude," Zack said. "Not bad looking, either."

The bronze statue was green like the Statue of Liberty, but the man's features were still easily discerned. He'd had a beard, a fine, straight nose, full lips, and hair that touched the collar of his pea coat. He looked like one of the heroes in Meg's books. She had been right – he looked like the little sailor on her kitchen wall.

Zack shivered. "It's so cold. Why don't we go get some cocoa?"

They went back to the sidewalk and Meg saw a large sign in the window of a card store saying they were closing early for Christmas Eve, and she suddenly remembered what Irma had said while they were looking at the painting.

"It's the door to the Christmas cottage," Irma had said. "It was painted by Molly Barton."

Meg held her breath. Many people painted doors and windows, but had Molly painted that door because she believed it would bring Colin home? Ethan said Molly had gone mad, so it would make sense that her desire for his return was so great it would cause delusions and create ideas of how to bring him back.

She pitied Molly. It must have been awful to love someone so much that it literally drove you insane.

As they walked toward a restaurant, she thought of Colin. He, too, was unable to rest, and had somehow conjured an image of himself on her kitchen wall. For a second, the thought that Molly might show up in her living room tonight made her shudder, but she kept her thoughts to herself. She didn't want to be alone tonight, and the boys were already freaked out.

"This place better have cocoa," Zack said as they entered the restaurant. "Or hot buttered rum."

"That sounds good," Ethan said.

They were shown to a table near a large Christmas tree and a fireplace with a roaring fire.

"We might as well have an early supper," Meg said.

"I don't mind cooking later," Ethan said.

"You can still cook later," Zack said. "Geez, it's only two in the afternoon."

"I know," Meg said. "It's just so nice here, so warm and cozy."

"We can have supper," Ethan said, "and I'll make something light for later on." Zack looked at him and pursed his lips. "Oh, get over it. We're Meg's guests and she wants an early supper."

"Fine, we'll have an early supper."

Meg had never noticed Zack's propensity for sarcasm before. Perhaps it was Ethan's presence that made him act like a spoiled kid, or was it her appearance? She didn't look like his Aunt Meg, so maybe he felt he didn't have to afford her the respect she deserved.

Whatever it was, she didn't like it, but she also wanted to keep the peace, so she kept these thoughts to herself. Ethan didn't seem to mind Zack's juvenile behavior, and that's all that really mattered.

After supper, they went home, sat on the sofa, and turned on the TV. Molly needed the distraction and she was trying to avoid looking at the painting, as if doing so would activate it like a time travel portal. They were all tired and soon the men fell asleep. Meg smiled at she looked from one to the other, and their peaceful expressions helped her relax and soon she, too, fell asleep.

12

Meg had written a story once where the heroine died and the hero would visit her grave every year on the anniversary of her death. As she woke up from her nap, Meg remembered that story and thought about Colin and Molly. Perhaps he was coming to pay homage to their great love, and would walk to the cemetery rather than climbing the hill to the cottage.

Meg noticed that Ethan, who had been sitting between them, was gone, and she got up and went to the kitchen. The little sailor was sitting on a bench near the entrance of the park, and she saw Ethan sitting at the table with his back to the wall.

"Hey," she said. "I have a question for you." She sat across from him. "Was Molly Brinker buried here?"

He shook his head. "She's in the family mausoleum in Boston."

Well, that blows that theory, Meg thought.

"Why?" Ethan asked.

"I just thought he might be coming to visit her grave."

"Instead of your cottage."

"Right."

"I don't believe he's coming here, Meg." Ethan looked at her. "You look younger."

"That doesn't make me feel better."

Zack walked in and looked at the stove. "I thought you were cooking."

"It's only four," Ethan said. "You ate two hours ago."

Zack sat in the empty seat and folded his arms on the table. He looked from one to the other and tapped his fingers on his arms.

"I want to see what happens tonight." Zack tapped louder as Ethan frowned. "I want to see if he shows up."

"And what will you do if he does?" Meg asked.

"I'll challenge him to a duel. I won't let him sweep you off your feet and carry you to the underworld."

"I don't think he's a pedophile," Ethan said, and then looked at Meg's face. "Sorry."

Zack sat back and bit his lower lip. "Well, that's true. You do look really young."

"How young?" Meg asked.

"Like around thirteen."

"If you don't stop..." Ethan clamped his mouth shut.

"You might disappear."

"That's not funny, Zack." He tweaked her nose. "Stop that!"

She hadn't realized it before, but now she noticed how much Zack reminded her of her brother, Eddie. She sat back and bit her lower lip.

"I'm just teasing you. You're such a baby."

"I'm your aunt!" she cried.

Now even Ethan was smiling, and tried to suppress it when he saw the tears on her cheeks.

"Look, Meg, I'm sure it's only temporary," Ethan said. "When tomorrow comes, you'll be back to your old self." Her eyes grew wide, and Ethan blushed. "Not old, just yourself."

Zack put his hand on hers. "I'm sorry for teasing you before. I seem to say that a lot since I've been here, but I really am sorry."

"What *is* going to happen?" she said softly.

"Nothing," Ethan said. "Nothing is going to happen. It's just some weird trick of the light is all." He looked at Zack. "Just a trick of the light, period."

"Right," Zack said. "And we'll be here with you so you don't have to be afraid of anything."

"And just what would the two of you do to stop him, huh?" She looked at Ethan. "Hit him with a frying pan?" She looked at Zack. "Tease him to death?"

Meg got up and ran to her bedroom and they heard her slam the door.

"I need some wine," Zack said.

"Amen," Ethan said.

Meg looked at her reflection in the bedroom mirror. She vaguely remembered the girl staring back at her as her pubescent self, but the familiarity didn't bring her any comfort. She was frightened, and had no frame of reference to make sense of it all. She didn't want to be with the boys, and stayed in her room for a long time. When she did go back to the kitchen, she forced a smile, and they smiled back.

"Sometimes we get carried away," Ethan said.

"I know," she said. "And you're sorry."

"I'd offer you some wine but I don't think it's a good idea considering," Zack said.

"That I'm thirteen-years-old."

"Exactly."

"I guess I could start cooking," Ethan said.

Meg and Zack watched him walk to the stove and both looked at the wall, too. The little sailor was still sitting on a bench near the park. He waved, and both Meg and Zack waved back.

13

The warmth of the hearth took the chill out of the room. They were watching *It's a Wonderful Life,* and when it was over they all looked at their cell phones.

"Well," Zack said, "it's an hour till midnight."

Meg felt her heart beating. "Yes it is."

"Why don't I make some cocoa?" Ethan asked.

"That's a good idea," Meg said.

While Ethan went to the kitchen, Meg and Zack watched the news, and they both kept glancing at the front door. Ethan brought them their cocoa and then went back for his, and that's when they heard something break in the kitchen.

They both got up and went to see what had happened. Ethan was staring at the wall with a broken mug at his feet.

"I'm sorry," he said. "I saw that guy move and I dropped the mug."

"Don't worry about the mug," Meg said. "It's old. Just don't cut your foot."

She went to the closet and took out a broom while Zack put a paper towel over the area to sop up the cocoa. Ethan couldn't take his eyes off the wall, but he had to move so Meg could sweep up the broken pieces. When she was done, she looked at the painting and saw the sailor smoking his pipe again.

"He shouldn't smoke so much," she said.

Zack looked at it, too. "It does smell good, though."

They all looked at the clock above the kitchen sink. It was ten to midnight.

Meg put her hand on Ethan's arm. "I don't think he means us any harm."

Ethan glared at her. "You talk like this is real or something. This isn't real. It can't be real. We're all caught up in some delusion."

"Now you know that's bullshit," Zack said. "This isn't a delusion."

"It has to be. There's no way that…that thing can be an 18th century sea captain."

"There's only one way to find out."

Zack walked past Ethan, put his coat on, and went to the front door.

"Wait, Zack," Meg said as she followed him. "Where are you going?"

"I'm going to town. I'm gonna see if he's sitting on that bench."

"But what if we're supposed to wait for him?" Meg said.

"You both sound crazy," Ethan said.

Ethan's voice quivered. Meg went to him and put her hands on his arms.

"Don't be afraid," she said.

"Come with me," Zack said to Ethan.

"Stop this," Meg said. "And get away from that door."

"Are you coming with me?" Zack said again.

Meg's cell phone alarm went off at midnight and they all jumped.

"I forgot I set that," she said, her nerves rattled and her hands shaking. Zack looked at Ethan, who nodded. "No. You said you wouldn't leave me here alone."

"If he's on his way here, we'll pass him on the hill," Zack said.

She wanted to follow them, but she couldn't move. It was as if her feet were frozen in place. They left and shut the door without another word.

Meg was about to yell for the boys but hesitated. The light in the room had dimmed, and she looked to her right. She saw soft golden light coming from around the edges of the door in the painting. She turned toward it and noticed that the painted doorknob was now a 3D object and she walked toward, put her hand on it, and it was warm.

Her lack of fear was odd considering how afraid Meg had been just seconds before, but somehow she knew that whatever was on the other side of that door would not harm her. Meg took a deep breath and turned the doorknob.

14

Meg pulled the door toward her and felt the sun on her face. Seagulls squawked overhead, and she squinted, put her hand over her eyes, and saw a bright blue sky. Morning glories climbed up each side of the door, and a large oak tree stood in front of the cottage.

Meg stepped out and looked toward town. She saw the rooftops of the shops and a dirt road leading down the hill. She walked toward the road and passed a copse of bushes where she and Maddie had spent the night when old Mary Spencer lived there.

Meg looked down and the ground looked closer. She was wearing the sneakers she'd worn when she was ten – a pair of white Keds covered in scuffmarks and dirt. She also recognized the shirt she had on as the one she'd picked out in Sears. It was a sleeveless, and she didn't like to tuck it into her madras Bermuda shorts.

Meg looked at her hands, and then her arms, and then ran her hand over the long ponytails lying on her shoulders. She was a girl again, and she began to run, feeling so free that she screamed at the top of her lungs, and then laughed as the wind blew back her hair and made her eyes water. If this was a dream, it was the best she'd ever had.

As she neared town, she heard the sound of a bell ringing from the church steeple. It was a perfect summer day, complete with biting flies, and Meg smacked one that landed on her leg. She was brushing it away as she walked, and when she looked up, she saw him standing at the entrance to the park.

Meg stopped and looked at him, and he looked at her. His eyes twinkled and he smiled broadly. It was Colin Brinker in the flesh, and he was delighted to see her.

"Why, you must be Meggie," he said.

Meggie. No one had called her that in years, and hearing it made her smile.

"Yes, I am."

"Well, I would have known you anywhere."

Without fear, she walked up to him and looked at his navy blue pea coat and his cap.

"Aren't you hot in that coat?" she asked.

He shook his head and winked.

"I never get too hot, my darlin'," he said. "So, why don't we take a walk?"

He held out his hand and she took it, and they walked toward the docks. The scent of salt water brought sweet memories of her childhood. Meg was lost in a reverie as they approached the docks and didn't see the little sailboat bobbing up and down beside the dock. She also didn't see the two children climbing out of it for her eyes were on the three-masted ship anchored miles away from land. She turned to ask Colin about it when she saw two familiar faces running toward her.

"Meggie!"

Tears filled her eyes as she ran toward them, running into arms she missed for so long. They all embraced, the boy and his two sisters, hugging each other tightly, and crying with joy.

"Oh, Meggie," the girl said. "I've missed you so."

"Oh, Maddie, you can't imagine how awful it's been without you."

"What about me?"

Meg looked at her brother. "I've missed you, too."

"Well, that's more like it."

"I can't believe you're both here," Meg said. "How did this happen?"

"We don't know. We found ourselves in that sailboat and Mr. Brinker told us we were going to have a grand surprise."

"Aye," Colin said. "And did I make good on my promise?" They all nodded and smiled at Colin. "So, off with you, then." Colin winked. "And don't forget to keep an eye on the sun."

The trio waved as they left him on the dock, and then they ran toward the town. All the old shops were there – the drug store with a soda fountain where they'd had malted milkshakes, the five and dime where they would buy boxes of chalk and draw on the sidewalk, and the movie house where they would watch movies for fifty cents. As they walked down the sidewalk, Maddie stopped in front of the drug store and looked at the magazine rack inside.

"Oh, that Paul McCartney is the cutest Beatle," she said. "He's so dreamy."

"I like him, too," Meg said.

"Well, we both can't have him. You can have George."

"But I don't want George."

"Well, you have to take him because Paul is mine."

"Then I'll take John."

Somewhere along the way, they'd lost Eddie, who had wandered off on his own adventure. The girls looked in each shop window and took turns imagining what it would be like if they were standing at their school bus stop and were spotted by the Beatles as they drove by.

"I'll bet Paul would ask me if I needed a ride," Maddie said. "And I'd smile and tell him I'd have to think about it."

"I'd go," Meg said.

"Oh, Meggie, you can't just go. You have to play hard to get."

"But I'd want to go."

"Well, then it's a good thing he's not for you."

They came to an older building where they used to play duckpin bowling.

"Come on," Maddie said, taking Meg's hand and pulling her inside.

The place was poorly lit but the duckpin alleys were illuminated. They walked up to one and Maddie grabbed a ball. They were smaller than bowling balls, and the pins were shorter, so when she rolled the ball down the alley, it went fast, and she scored a strike.

"Yay!" she yelled, and turned to smile at Meg, who suddenly longed to hold her sister and never let go.

Eddie was at the other end of the bowling alley, and Meg and Maddie watched him score strike after strike.

"He always likes to show off," Maddie said.

"That's because I'm the best," he said.

Maddie rolled her eyes. "He always says that."

"He is good," Meg said.

"Well, yeah, but he doesn't have to say it all the time."

Some moments in life are too sweet, too good, and the desire to hold onto them takes precedence over everything else. Meg was having one of those moments. She knew this dream would have to end, but her desire to stay with them was overwhelming. She'd lost them once and couldn't bear the thought of losing them again.

"I want to stay with you," she said.

Maddie was throwing another ball and had her back to Meg. When she was done, she looked at her sister with tears in her eyes.

"You know you can't, Meggie."

"Why not? Why can't I decide what I want to do?"

Maddie took her hand. "Because it's not your time."

She looked in Meg's eyes and the warmth and love Meg saw made her more determined to stay.

"Well, I say it is my time."

"It's not up to you, sweetie." Maddie came closer. "Besides, I need you to look after Zack."

Maddie knew. She understood that this was a gift, a day with her siblings designed to bring them peace. Meg hadn't been there when her siblings passed. She wasn't there to hold their hands and say goodbye. She never imagined that they had missed that, too.

"We are here to say goodbye, Meggie."

"But I don't want to say goodbye."

Meggie wrapped her arms around her sister's waist and cried into her chest. Her sobs brought Eddie, who put his arms around them both.

"It's okay," he said. "Stop blubbering."

"She needs this, Eddie. She's our baby sister. Be nice."

As she nestled in the loving arms of her family, Meg felt a release, a letting go; not of the love, but of the pain. No matter what separated them, they would always be siblings.

They left the bowling alley, stood on the sidewalk, and looked at the sky.

"The sun's going down," Eddie said. He went to Meg and looked into her eyes. "I'll see ya, Meggie. Don't take any wooden nickels."

"I won't, Eddie."

He came and hugged her, and as they pulled apart, she saw tears in his eyes.

"See you in another life," he said.

His voice quivered, and then he looked toward the docks and began to run.

"He never could handle the mushy stuff," Maddie said.

Now the sisters were left alone, and Meg again felt the need to hold on to Maddie. She took her hand and squeezed it.

"Are you sure I can't stay with you?" Meg asked.

"You'll be okay now," Maddie said. "You'll be okay."

Meg hugged her tightly. "I'll never stop missing you."

"I know."

"I can't say it."

"Then I'll say it for both of us. Goodbye, my sweet sister."

As she watched Maddie walk away, Meg was grateful to her. She and Eddie had given Meg the only thing she wanted for Christmas, a chance to see them both one more time. The sky was streaked with lavender and pink hues, and as she walked back to the dirt road leading to the cottage, she saw the tiny sailboat heading out to sea.

15

Meg didn't remember going to bed, but when she woke up, she was tucked in the way her mother had tucked her in every night. She thought she could smell the scent of her mother's perfume, but it brought a sense of peace instead of tears.

She sat and stretched, and she was sad to find that all her aches and pains had returned, along with her wrinkled hands.

"Couldn't I have kept my teenage joints?" she asked out loud.

She stood and smelled coffee. Ethan must be up and making breakfast. She put on her robe and left the room.

Zack was still huddled under the blankets on the pullout sofa and he grunted when she said, "Good morning. Merry Christmas."

Ethan was at the stove making pancakes and he smiled when he saw her.

"You're back! Did you sleep well?" he asked.

"I did, and you?"

"After we came back last night, we found you asleep on the sofa, so he carried you to bed. He kept waking up and thinking he heard someone at the door. I think he was disappointed when the Captain didn't show up." She sat at the table and he looked at her. "Look at the wall."

She looked and saw that the picture had vanished.

"The little sailor is gone," he said. "You want some coffee?"

"Aren't you curious about why he came?" she asked.

"Not really. If I can't figure something out, I stop thinking about it."

"You can do that?"

"It's what I've always done."

She wasn't sure he'd believe her if she told him what had happened during the night anyway. Ethan seemed content not to know, so she decided to keep it to herself. She didn't know about Zack, though. Would he want to know his mother came to her and not him?

No, she thought.

It would hurt him. It would make him think she didn't love him as much, and that wasn't true. This had nothing to do with Zack. It was her gift. She had been devastated when she missed her sister's last breaths, but Zack had been there. He'd been able to say goodbye.

"So what are we doing today?" she asked.

Ethan brought her a plate of pancakes.

"We could go for a ride, or go to Boston to look at the store windows." He smiled. "I've already got everything ready for dinner. All we have to do is heat it up."

"How?"

"I got up early."

Another hour passed before Zack got out of bed and they decided that they would go to Boston, take a ride through the old neighborhood, and spend the day reminiscing about Maddie and Uncle Eddie. They left right after Zack got dressed and Ethan packed their lunches.

When they returned to Port Revere, they ate Ethan's dinner, drank wine, and the boys told Meg how they met. They also told her she always had a room at their place if she wanted to visit California.

The next day as they drove away, Meg waved at them and sighed. Of all the Christmases past and future, this was by far the best she'd ever had.

"Thank you," she said as she looked at the sea. "I'll see you in another life."

The End

And now, a sample from

LIBBY THE
PSYCHIC DOG

A Series by A.L. Jambor

EPISODE 1

Allow me to introduce myself. My name is Percival Plep and I am a Lord of the Realm. Well, perhaps not at present, but I started out my life as a young man full of vigor and ready to take on the world. My father, 8th Lord of Pembroke, had prepared me for a life of hard work and service. As a member of the House of Lords, he would shape the future of his beloved homeland, this blessed plot, this realm, this England. I had my work cut out for me, let me tell you. But that was in another life, one that was cut short by a the war to end all wars. I died in a trench in France, a Hun's bullet in my chest. Where I went after that I can't recall, but one day I woke to find myself surrounded by the most adorable puppies I'd ever seen.

It took a while to acclimate myself to exactly where I was. Everything surrounding me was enormous. I had to look up, and when I saw the giant face of a woman staring down at me, I nearly lost consciousness. I watched as the other puppies went to the fence separating the woman from them.

They stood on their hind legs, wagging their little tails, and whimpering like fools. I hadn't yet noticed my appendages. When I did, the dawning realization that I, too, was a puppy, well, it, to say the least, upset me.

I opened my mouth to protest and to ask the woman where I was, but I couldn't command my tongue to speak words. Instead, a whiny growl emitted from my mouth and she looked at me with a quizzical expression.

"You finally woke up," she said. Her hand came toward me and I backed away, but she was too swift. She had me in her hand and was stroking my head. Her eyes looked into mine and I felt, well, oddly comforted. She had a nice smile and her hands were warm. "We didn't know if you would make it," she said. "I'm glad to see you're all right."

She placed me back on the floor. A dog appeared behind her and she bent down to pat its head. I recognized it as a Rat Terrier of sorts, maybe in combination with another breed. It was taller and wider than the puppies and I came to the conclusion that it must be their mother, which meant it was my mother, too. That revelation sent me into a tizzy. If this was the mother, and I the puppy, than I would be feeding off her...oh dear. The woman lifted Mother over the fence and she lay down.

The puppies rushed to her and began nudging her swollen teats. I found the whole display embarrassing, but as I watched the puppies lulled into blissful silence, cuddled side by side, I had the strangest urge to join them. I held back, determined to keep my dignity, but my stomach grumbled, mocking me. I felt myself being propelled forward until I was near her, and saw an available nipple. With great trepidation, I drew closer, sniffed it, and found its scent pleasing. I then latched on like a hungry wolf, taken on the wings of delight to a place I could only have imagined before. This truly was heaven. Before I knew it, I, too, was lulled into a state of blissful silence and fell sleep with the teat in my mouth.

Much to my embarrassment, I awoke in the same position. Mother was licking my head. I am loath to admit it felt wonderful, her tongue lapping my cranium, and the closeness of her warm body. My brothers and sisters were tumbling around, playing and barking to their heart's content. I wondered where the human had gone to. Didn't their jabbering bother her? It would have bothered me in my human state, I tell you.

When Mother was assured I was spic and span, she nudged me to join the others. Rather than enter the fray, I observed them. I would have to learn how to act like one of them, for the sake of the humans, and also how to respond to other dogs. Their culture fascinated me. I watched them lift their tails in response to the nearness of another's nose and found the habit repulsive. I also watched as they relieved themselves by squatting. I followed suit. It was the only way to accomplish the deed. This particular activity would soon cause me a great deal of angst. But that was yet to come.

One day, after many weeks of frolicking in the penned area, the woman, whom I was to learn was called Edna, brought another human to the pen. The man was very tall and towered over us. My sisters cowered near my mother, who growled defensively. My brothers, however, went right to the fence and barked. The man smiled.

"I'm looking for a male," he said.

"Oh, we have three," Edna said.

She pointed to my brothers and he asked to "see" one. She picked up the one I had been calling Cedric and handed him to the man. The man inspected Cedric by looking at his hindquarters. For a moment I thought he would sniff it, but he didn't, though it would have been jolly fun if he had.

"May I see that one?" he asked, pointing to Ernest.

She lifted Ernest and placed him in the man's hand while we all sniffed Cedric, who had been returned to the pen.

"I like this little guy," he said as Ernest licked his face, making an utter display of himself. Frankly,

I was embarrassed for him.

"Are you sure? You can spend a little more time with him if you'd like."

"No," he said. "This guy seems to like me."

They walked away taking Ernest with them. It was then that I realized I wasn't going to spend the rest of my life with my family. Yes, they were now my family, and the thought of leaving Mother made me sad. Unlike my human mother, she was quiet and warm. I liked cuddling with her at night when the sounds of the house made my brothers and sisters nervous. They were perk up and growl, but I knew what they were - sounds of the house settling. I tried to tell them, but they couldn't understand me. This inability to communication would continue to plague me throughout my life.

When Edna returned, she bore a sad expression.

"I'm sorry, baby," she said. She came over and stroked Mother's head. "I want to keep them all, too, but we have to let them go."

I shuddered. I thought of the kind of person she would sell me to and I started to shake. I knew how people treated dogs. Images of my brothers and sisters chained to a house in the back yard, shivering in the cold, full of fleas and other nasty things filled my head. I tried to push it away, but to no avail. I felt so sad, in fact, that I ran to Mother and burrowed my head under her soft belly. I couldn't bear to look at Edna, whose betrayal had brought the terror that now filled my heart.

After a spell, I came out from under Mother. Edna was gone and I wondered where she found the people she sold us to. Maybe she wouldn't be able to find a buyer for me, and then I would stay with her. Better the enemy you know, old chap, I told myself. It was at that moment I noticed Cedric do something that would change my life forever. He lifted his leg to relieve himself. I had to go myself and went to the spot where he had gone. I lifted my leg but instead of creating a stream that went away from my body, I felt a dribble go down my leg. Cedric was watching me. If a canine could laugh, he would have been doubled over. I couldn't understand why I hadn't been able to imitate what he'd done. Mother came over and began cleaning me. She cleaned my nether regions and it was then that I understood why I had been unable to send the urine away from my body.

As I laid down, I went to lick myself. Up until then, I hadn't paid much attention to my own body. I had let my mother bathe me, but when I looked at myself that day, I noticed the absence of a male appendage. My heart began to beat faster. Oh, it couldn't be true, could it? Had the gods conspired to ruin me completely? As the overwhelming shock subsided, I decided I would have to accept my fate, for I not only had I been reincarnated as a dog, I was, in fact, a female.

There are five books in the *Libby the Psychic Dog* series. They are available on Amazon. I have provided the link for Episode 1 here.

ABOUT THE AUTHOR

A.l. Jambor

A.L. Jambor began writing in 2010. Inspired by a photo of her granddaughter, she wrote the harrowing story of a pharmaceutical nightmare called But the Children Survived. The book was a hit, and she wrote more books, novellas, and shorts.

Amy's love of animals is reflected in her stories. Several books feature domestic pets or service or therapy animals, as in the case of Libby the Psychic Dog. She supports local rescue shelters and contributes to national organizations in the fight against animal abuse. Amy encourages her fans to help stop the exploitation of innocent animals in puppy mills and supports no-kill shelters and rescues.

Amy lives in Florida. She shares her home with two cats, Sammy and Puff. Her favorite genre is mystery, with historical fiction coming in at a close second. In her spare time, A.L. Jambor enjoys reading mysteries and solving puzzles.

BOOKS BY THIS AUTHOR

Whispers In The Dark

A woman named Mari suffers a traumatic brain injury and wakes up with the ability to see ghosts. Not just any ghosts, but those involved in a murder. The accused claims that she didn't kill the young, pregnant woman, and after looking into the crime, Mari begins to doubt her guilt. She agrees to help the ghosts bring the culprit to justice.

A Lethal Legacy: A Victorian Murder Mystery

Lady Felicity Armstrong is orphaned and broke. She must find a place to live and start a new life. After she settles in a small beach community of Tolwich. Felicity makes the best of things and is content with her life, until her old housekeeper invites her to visit. The visit goes well, until the housekeeper is found dead.

Where's Audrey?

Aunt Audrey is missing, and her young niece, Mel, thinks she's been murdered.

The Secret Of Truelock Manor

This family saga begins in 1705. The Truelock family begin their legacy with a small cabin on Cape Cod built by Jedediah, the patriarch who abandons his wife and two sons for the open seas. . The sons, Lawrence and Homer, were as different as night and day, but together they build on their father's small fortune. But it's Lawrence's son, Stephen, who becomes the center of this story, as he navigates the world, and falls in love with the only woman he will ever love, Mercy.

Dangerous Stranger

In 1957, Harold Bender was tried and convicted for the murder of Brenda Stern. Sixty years later, his public defender becomes convinced that Harold was wrongly convicted. He sets out to prove it with the help of his grandson and a trooper from the PA highway patrol. Their investigation leads them to Alaska, where they learn that the truth behind Brenda's murder is far worse than the wrongful conviction of an innocent man.

The Silver Stag

1986 - James Huxley, the only son of the Earl of Dorley, loves to spend his time in the attic of the manor house reading fantasy books. In 1986, his summer plans include rereading the Lord of the Rings trilogy, so when his father tells him they will have a guest for the summer, and that he expects James to entertain her, James balks, until he sees their guest – a lovely girl his age named Mia. At sixteen, James has never had a girlfriend, but he falls head over heels for the seductive American.

But The Children Survived

A post apocalyptic story of a group of children who survive a pharmaceutical accident. Who is responsible for the disaster? And how did the children avoid death?

The House On The Shore: A Paranormal Mystery

The 1953 death of Bertram Warren was ruled an accident, but Detective Jerry Keating believed Bertram was murdered by his young wife, Cora. He also believed that their daughter, ten-year-old Meghan, saw what happened. When Jerry tried to question the girl, her mother called the chief of police, and they told Jerry to back off. Some sixty years later, Cora dies, and she leaves her house on the shore to her only living relative, a young woman named Mariah Kimball. Soon, past residents of the house start visiting Mariah, along with a detective who wants to find out what happened to Cora's husband.

Sisters And Whiskers

Emma Novak owns a demanding cat, one of a bonded pair that lost his brother when Emma lost her husband to a brain aneurysm. She has drawn comfort from the cat's presence, but a year after her husband passed away, Emma is still fighting the urge to stay in bed and hide her head under the covers. She also has a sister who wants her to sell their mother's house, and an uncle who is fighting a sale. After all, he's lived there for two hundred years.

The Ladies Of Lavender Lane

Angry divorcee Alice Beck isn't looking forward to her first Christmas alone. Fortunately, Alice has inherited a house from her great-aunt, and it's the perfect place to spend the holidays. Alice plans to read her romance novels, but something, or someone, interrupts her plans. Will Alice have the best Chrismas of her life, or the worst?

Libby The Psychic Dog

The first in a series of five books featuring Libby, a pudgy terrier who inner life is very special. She is the reincarnation of a WWI soldier named Lord Percival Plep, and she spends her time solving mysteries and eating with her beloved Mama.